Basics of Business Management series

A Concise Guide to
Basics of
Business Management

(All in a nutshell)

W0008040

A.S. Srinivasan

Clever Fox
PUBLISHING

Chennai • Bangalore

CLEVER FOX PUBLISHING
Chennai, India

Published by CLEVER FOX PUBLISHING 2023
Copyright © A.S.Srinivasan 2023

All Rights Reserved.
ISBN: 978-93-56482-15-9

Introduction

This booklet will be of use to all those who are interested in the field of Business Management. If you are a practising manager or an entrepreneur, this could serve as a refresher. If you have recently taken up a managerial position, this will be a useful reference book for you to look at some of the concepts mentioned here. If you are a student or a person interested to know the basics of management, this will serve the purpose of a guidebook.

This booklet is brief but comprehensive, outlining all the major management concepts and practices in all functional areas. As a manager in today's highly competitive and dynamic business environment, you need to

1. Develop the capability to look at your organisation's business holistically

2. Become familiar with major concepts and practices in all functional areas of management

3. Understand the integrated nature of your business, the interconnectedness of various functions and the impact of your individual and departmental decisions and actions on the total operations of the company and

4. Have the urge to develop yourself further to meet the challenges of today and tomorrow

Hopefully, this booklet will help you embark on this journey of life-long learning.

I have primarily relied on various management books by leading authors in compiling all the concepts presented here which I gratefully acknowledge. I claim no originality or ownership of these

1

ideas. I have gathered these over the years I was serving in academics. I have appended a list of primary references and have mentioned the names of original thinkers and writers in my text at appropriate places. There are many more that are in public domain which I have used in presenting these contents.

All these classic concepts have been mentioned very briefly and need further study for greater understanding. This is in no way a textbook. It is just a window to the field of management. This booklet will have served its purpose if it arouses your curiosity to know more on any topic or concept you are interested in. I look forward to receiving your comments and feedback.

Welcome to a short journey through this fascinating field of management!

A.S. Srinivasan   **October, 2022**

Contents

Block 1: Introduction to Business and Management

This section broadly defines what business is all about and what managers do to look after the affairs of an organisation. The topics covered are:

1. Basic purpose of business
2. Business model
3. The managerial job
4. Making money

Block 2: Organisations - The basic units of business

Generally, organisations are the basic unit in business. This section covers:

1. Organisation basics
2. Organisational culture, structure, systems and processes
3. Developing competitive strategies

Block 3: Marketing Management

The primary objective of any business is to deliver customer value better than competition, while making a profit. This section covers the following topics to be considered in developing customer orientation:

1. Defining and understanding customers and markets
2. Segmentation, targeting and positioning
3. Managing elements of the marketing mix
4. Managing customer relations, managing brands and communication
5. Developing marketing strategies

Block 4: Human Resources Management

Managing people is integral part of every manager's job. This section covers the following critical areas:

1. Understanding human behaviour
2. Leadership essentials
3. Managing performance and development
4. Managing change

Block 5: Financial Management

In business, all activities are measured in money terms and performance is evaluated based on financial information. This section gives the required background in finance covering the following:

1. Understanding financial statements
2. Financial ratio analysis
3. Understanding costs and budgets
4. Understanding shareholder value

Block 6: Managing Operations and the Supply Chain

Operations is the backbone of any business organisation and managing the entire supply chain is of critical importance to business success. This section covers the basics of operations and supply chain management under:

1. Managing the steady state in Operations and support functions
2. Continuous performance improvement
3. Managing the supply chain
4. Key emerging technologies

Block 1: An introduction to Business and Management

1.1 The basic purpose of any business is to make profits and to add on to the wealth of the promoters by fulfilling a perceived customer need. Even for government and not-for-profit organisations, making a surplus (profit) which is income less expenses, is essential to maintain current operations, invest and grow for the future.

1.2 Apart from promoters and shareholders, there are other stakeholders interested in the profitable running of the organisation. Various stakeholder groups are:

- Owners
- Employees
- Customers
- Creditors
- Suppliers
- Local community and society at large
- Government

Hence fulfilling the expectations of all these stakeholders is the job of top management. This calls for developing a holistic view of business and a systems approach to balance their conflicting demands.

1.3 There is no one universal way for running a business successfully. It all depends on the nature of business, ownership, the environment in which the company is operating, opportunities and problems faced by the firm at various stages of growth etc. Thus, firms are classified based on all these factors.

1.4　We need to measure the performance of the company on a continuing basis so that we can take corrective steps when necessary. Financial measures were largely used earlier since the dominant view was that business of business was "business only" or to "maximise profits only". But as we just saw, there are other stakeholders whose interests have also to be fulfilled. While several new measures apart from financial measures have been developed, a broad framework will cover the following:

- Effectivity: Are we doing the right thing? Are we moving in the right direction?

- Efficiency: Are we doing it the right way? Are we using our resources efficiently?

- Economy: Are we doing it at minimal costs?

- Ethics: Are we doing right? Are we adhering to the moral and ethical standards of society?

- Equity: Are we treating all our employees on an equitable basis?

2.　Business model:

2.1　We will use the terms- business, organisation, firm, company, corporation etc. interchangeably to connote the business entity.

2.2　Every business works on a business model stated explicitly or implied, to fulfill its objectives. The basic business model consists of:

- What is the firm's offering?

- What are the benefits and value the firm is offering to its customers?

6

- To whom is the offering made? Target customer groups of the firm

- How is the company structured to utilise its resources and capabilities to deliver this value? This is analysed by using a concept called value chain which indicates value added by each component of the firm

- What are the financial results? This considers the profits generated based on its income streams, expenses and cost structure and investments made.

2.3   A firm's competitive strategy is based on its business model plus its competitive environment. Thus, firms have to do all these- offer greater value to customers than competition while incurring lower costs on a continuous basis. This is the crux of creating sustainable competitive advantage.

3.   The job of a manager:

3.1   Companies are run by individual managers who form the Management team, and we look at what managers ought to do and what they actually do. We look at the managerial job in terms of the roles they play, the process of managing and the contexts in which they manage.

3.2   Rational view of managing: Managers should

- forecast and plan
- organise
- command
- co-ordinate and
- control the firm's operations

3.3   Reality of managing: In reality, managers are hard pressed for time to take rational decisions for several problems and hence their decisions are based on bounded rationality. This means that they take decisions that are satisficing rather than maximising.

3.4   Managerial problems also tend to be complex with multiple causes and effects and "people" dimension has to be considered while seeking solutions to problems. This is reality.

3.5   The structured approach to problem solving and decision making consists of following steps:

   •   Step 1: Identification and definition

   •   Step 2: Setting objectives

   •   Step 3: Option appraisal and decision making

   •   Step 4: Communication and implementation

   •   Step 5: Monitoring and control

3.6   Since today's business problems are often complex, we need to look at other approaches involving creative thinking. There are several techniques for creative problem solving and these involve lateral thinking, brainstorming etc.

3.7   Ultimately if essence of management work is to make things happen, managers need to plan and control all activities and take their people with them.

3.8   Today's dynamic business environment is dictated by

   •   Explosive growth in Information and Communication Technologies (ICT) and impact of the digital world on newer technologies

- Rapidly expanding liberalisation and globalisation of international trade as well as 'protectionist' measures by all major countries
- Changing demographics
- Discriminating customers
- Changing work practices like working from home, part-time etc. resulting in declining life-long employment
- Increasingly demanding owners and all stakeholders
- Uncertainties in the global economies
- Continuing environmental degradation
- And today, the ongoing catastrophic Covid pandemic that has totally altered the ways we all have been living

3.9   These have the following impact on managers:

- Increased workload and long working hours
- Increased span of control which means that managers have more people reporting to them
- Changing nature of role, from specialist to generalist
- Emphasis on performance leading to less security, more mobility and no life-long employment
- Greater freedom or "empowerment" which results in greater responsibilities and hence need to know more and act more
- Changing the very way we used to work- virtual offices and meetings replacing traditional physical offices and face-to-face meetings

Hence old ways of doing things may not always hold good. There is a need for continuous learning and development.

4.   Making money:

4.1   Basically, managers need to know how their firms make money or profits. Making money involves several important steps as follows:

- Forecasting the future

- Making necessary investments

- Bringing all the resources together to make the company's products/services and marketing these offerings to targeted customers while controlling costs and maxmising incomes

All these are critical in ensuring profitable operations of the company.

4.2   Most importantly, people make things happen and managing human resources is basic to managing for profits.

4.3   In a larger sense, making money in a business involves "systems thinking"- thinking of the whole and its components and putting them all together to achieve synergy whereby the sum total is bigger than just the sum of individual components.

4.4   While the emphasis has shifted from maximising profits only to fulfilling the demands of all stakeholders, companies need to optimize their profits and generate surplus to meet present and future money requirements.

Block 2: Organisations – The basic units of business

1. Organisation basics:

1.1 Organisations are people and all organisations have

- People
- Objectives and
- Structure.

They achieve their common objectives by bringing people and other resources together. The sum total of all individual efforts is greater than just the sum of individual efforts which is called synergy. This is done first by differentiating the activities of the organisation and then by integrating these efforts.

1.2 Thus, the two key issues in managing in organisations are:

- How to balance differentiation and co-ordination?
- How to create a unified organisational identity through a common purpose?

This is because the differentiated sub-units within the organisation have different perspectives and concerns.

1.3 In the past and even now, many organisations are structured in a highly hierarchical manner. But with tasks becoming more specialised and complicated, modern organisations tend to be flatter and are driven by self-managing teams. Taking this further, today's organisations are networked with their collaborative value chain partners starting with raw material suppliers to final dealers or customer contact points where sales are made, and goods and services delivered.

1.4 Organisations even within an industry will vary based on the following:
- Size
- Technology used
- Location
- Type of ownership etc.

1.5 Organisational design involves differentiating tasks to individual jobs or roles and then coordinating and controlling these individual jobs.

2. Culture, structure, systems and processes:

2.1 An organisation's culture is seen through "the way things are done here". It develops over time based on the promoters' and senior people's values, ideologies, beliefs and assumptions and gets manifested in ways of working and reporting, stories, rituals, language, office layout etc.

2.2 Models to describe culture are based on how decisions are made, work gets done and feedback given etc. like task culture, bureaucratic culture etc.

2.3 To meet the external challenges, today organisations attempt to bring in cultural changes with themes like:
- Customer orientation
- Quality orientation
- Cost orientation
- People orientation etc.

2.4 Organisations are structured in several ways to carry out the tasks. some major dimensions defining the structure are:
- Span of control

- Hierarchy
- Specialisation
- Unity of command etc.

2.5 Organisations are generally structured along
- Functional lines like Manufacturing, Marketing, Finance
- Product lines
- Geographical lines or
- A combination of these.

2.6 All we can is that there is no one best way of structuring an organisation. Among other things, it depends on size, strategy, technology etc.

2.7 Organisations are driven by their values. Values define their mission (why), aims or goal (what) and objectives and targets (how).

2.8 These days, organisational ethics is a major subject of study and individual mangers have to resolve their ethical dilemmas by balancing their individual, company and society's values.

2.9 Organisations are also moving beyond making profits alone as their primary objective and are taking part in resolving societal issues. To sustain on a long-term basis, they need to be ethical by doing the right things as per society's standards.

2.10 Organisations can be seen as systems converting certain inputs (resources) to desired outputs (products, services etc.). Today more and more organisations concentrate on their core capabilities (what they are best at doing) while outsourcing other activities. This involves make or buy decisions.

2.11 If organisation's vision defines why we are doing this, aims and goals specify what we want to achieve, then processes set out how we are going to do this. Processes have a specific sequence of activities with clearly defined inputs and outputs and time.

3. **Developing competitive strategies:**

3.1 Strategy is all about matching resources of the organisation with opportunities available in the external environment to fulfill the business objectives of the firm. Thus, strategy involves analysing and understanding the dynamic external environment as well organisation's own resources and capabilities.

3.2 The chosen strategy sets the direction, determines the nature, scope and domain of firm's activities, evaluates success of these activities, makes further resource commitments and develops capabilities to meet emerging challenges and opportunities.

3.3 Strategy making consists of three major processes: strategic analysis, strategic choice and strategy implementation. It starts with developing the mission based on an analysis of its multiple stakeholders' expectations creating value for all of them.

3.4 Normally it is assumed that by pursuing profit as the single important objective, organisations will be able to meet the expectations of all stakeholders since fulfilling them depends on making profits. However, there have been cases where single minded approaches to profit maximization at the cost of some other stakeholder requirements, have led to adverse impact on the reputation and standing of the firm.

3.5 The process starts with an analysis of macro business environment and the industry environment in which the firm operates. A useful framework in studying the macro environment is called STEEP (sociological, technological, economic, environmental and political) analysis.

3.6 Using another framework known as five forces framework developed by Mr. Michael Porter, we analyse the industry environment to understand the competitive nature of industry in which the firm is operating. This helps in understanding the key success factors to succeed. The five forces listed are:

- Supplier power
- Buyer power
- Threat of substitutes
- Threat of new entry and
- Industry rivalry

3.7 We then move on to analyse the resources and capabilities of the organisation to develop its competitive advantage given the key success factors to succeed in the chosen industry. While resources are the basic building blocks, it is the ability of the firm to employ these resources together to produce better results called capabilities that give the organisation necessary competitive advantage. When this competitive advantage takes care of future competition as well, it becomes sustainable and that is what firms work on.

3.8 Competitive advantage could emerge from external developments like demographic shifts, changes in customer demand, technology etc. It can also result from the organisation's superior creative and innovative capability coupled with agile or quick and effective response to external changes.

3.9   Companies could adopt a cost advantage route or a differentiation advantage route in selecting its broad strategy. The capabilities required for each of these broad strategies are different.

3.10 We can use the concept of value chain developed by Mr. Michael Porter to identify areas where the organisation can develop cost advantage. Under this, each major activity in the organisation is analysed to arrive at the value added at that stage.

3.11 For pursuing diffentiation advantage, the organisation needs to study the customer segments and their preferences to offer a product/service that will give greater value to the chosen customer segment than competition.

3.12 In implementing strategy, organisations need to constantly evaluate at what stage of growth the industry is in and technological and other developments that are taking place or likely to take place and keep acquiring necessary resources and capabilities. Thus, strategy implementation is dynamic.

3.13 McKinsey's 7S framework is an organisational analysis model involving 7 aspects of an organisation that are to be considered in implementation of strategy. These are:
- Structure
- Systems
- Style
- Staff
- Skills
- Strategy
- Shared values which dictate the other factors

3.14 In multi-product, multi-divisional corporate setting, organisations could expand their activities either through forward/backward integration in the same industry, entering into new geographic markets or get into offering new products or services called diversification.

3.15 In the last decades, strategy making in organisations has been influenced by following developments:

- More emphasis on resource-based view leading to developing resources and capabilities than merely reacting to external changes

- Ensuring sustainable competitive advantage by offering add-on products and services to an already established large loyal customer base, called creating network effects

- Creating new strategic space in existing industries through better understanding of various customer segments' preferences and positioning products/services to meet these preferences. This has led to new strategic approaches like the 'blue ocean strategy" as outlined by Profs. W. Chan Kim and Renee Mauborgne and "reverse positioning" as developed by companies like IKEA and Starbucks.

- Using more refined financial analysis to estimate the financial outcome of various options.

- Greater reliance on emerging new technologies for data collection, analysis and decision making

3.16 Ultimately developing and implementing successful strategies on a sustainable basis depend largely on the quality of company/corporate leadership.

Block 3: Marketing Management

1. Defining and understanding customers and markets:

1.1 If business is all about finding out customer needs and fulfilling them at a profit, marketing plays a central role in this endeavour.

1.2 As the economies grew from a product and producer-led state to customer driven economies due to development and changes in general economic conditions, technologies, demographics, customer expectations and competition, firms evolved to become more and more market and customer oriented.

1.3 Marketing derives its principles and practices from sciences like economics, psychology, anthropology etc. to understand customer behaviour, competition, relationship between demand, supply, price etc.

1.4 There are regulations in marketing area to protect consumer interests and ensure fair and free competition. However, in reality there are no perfect markets due to resources and information asymmetry and companies exploit this to their advantage.

1.5 At a macro level, we analyse the external environment and competition and then move on to understand the consumer. The primary function of marketing is to choose a customer segment, find out their needs and wants and fulfill them by offering the customer greater value than competition. Only by doing this, firms can create and sustain competitive advantage.

1.6 Several forecasting tools and techniques are used to forecast present and future market potential for the firm's offerings and also predict future consumer wants and preferences based on emerging technologies.

1.7 To succeed in this marketing effort, firms need to understand the drivers of consumer behaviour and gain insight into customer preferences. They study the decision-making process of consumers and factors that influence their decision making.

1.8 This is done through using marketing research techniques for developing marketing tactics (short term, specific actions) and strategies (long term, holistic actions).

1.9 Broadly marketing research uses both qualitative and quantitative techniques to understand consumer behaviour and make quantitative forecasts on market potential, market share etc. We also use primary (direct research with consumers) and secondary (often published data) resources to collect information.

1.10 There are special tools and techniques to find out about consumer perceptions about company's and competitors' offerings to arrive at marketing decisions.

2. Segmentation, Targeting and Positioning:

2.1 Armed with these customer/market insights, firms move on to develop their marketing strategies. The first steps in this process are segmentation, targeting and positioning. Here the firm decides on which customer groups (segments) it wants to address and finalises its product/service offerings that will satisfy best, the needs of the chosen segments.

2.2 The firm's offerings may go directly to the end consumer in which case it is called B to C marketing. When the products go to another firm or business as a part of its offering to the final customer, it is called B to B marketing.

2.3 Several factors are considered in the segmentation exercise in both cases. Demographic, psychographic, geographic and behavioural factors are considered.

2.4 Firms decide on their target segments based on their attractiveness and their own capabilities to meet the requirements of the chosen segments.

2.5 Firms position their offerings in the minds of the consumers to ensure that their offerings offer them the best value in terms of physical, emotional and self-expressive benefits, relationships, access, service and overall experience.

2.6 Studying the external environment and firm's own resources and capabilities, Understanding the customer and his/her buying behaviour and competition and choosing and targeting the appropriate customer segments (Targeting) and Positioning the company's products/services in the minds of these customers as offering the best value in terms of functional and emotional benefits- these are the basic steps in company's marketing strategy.

3. Managing elements of the marketing mix:

3.1 A time-tested approach to implementing the marketing strategy of the company is managing the marketing mix elements. Though of late this approach is criticised for its focus on supplier's point of view, it still remains the basis for most marketing decisions since it starts with understanding the customer.

3.2 Generally four factors called the 4 Ps- Product, Price, Place and Promotion make the marketing mix. An additional three factors- People, Processes and Physical evidence have been added to cover services offering as well.

Product:

3.3 While all offerings from any company have both product and service elements, there are certain features which distinguish primarily service offerings like hospitality, travel, entertainment, health services, financial services etc. Among other features, customers cannot see, touch, feel and experience a service before it is offered. Thus, services are intangible. Also, since they are offered and consumed at the same time, they cannot be stored for future use. These make the human or People element along with the Process of offering (the promptness with which the purchase process is completed) and Physical evidence (the ambience in which purchase takes place) important in the marketing mix for services.

3.4 A concept known as product life cycle is useful in arriving at suitable product strategy. The product life cycle consists of following stages:

- Introduction
- Growth
- Maturity and
- Decline

The product strategy varies at each stage.

3.5 To meet ever-increasing profit objectives, companies need to constantly innovate and come out with new offerings giving even greater value to customers and phase out old, matured products. This process of new product development and creative destruction is part of company's profit evolution.

3.6 Companies will have to look at the benefits customers look for while designing and creating their product features. As they say, features are what companies provide and benefits are what customer sees. In fact, by gaining customer insight, companies should plan ahead to foresee emerging customer needs and wants, to stay ahead of competition. Recent advances of Apple iPhones may be a case in point.

3.7 Companies adopt this differentiation strategy by creating brand identities for their offerings to capture the top-of the mind space among customers. Thus, brand image consists of functional, emotional, and other intangible benefits.

Price:

3.8 While costing is in the domain of finance, pricing falls under marketing. This demonstrates the interconnected-ness of business functions.

3.9 You need to look at your costs, competitors' prices and customer expectations while fixing the selling price of your product. Thus, pricing strategies may be cost-related, market (customer)-related or competition-related.

3.10 The old practice of cost-based pricing is often on the way out. To compete effectively, companies go for customer/market-related pricing and control their costs to maintain their profitability.

3.11 Other factors like organisation's objectives, its capabilities and market potential and market share of its products dictate pricing strategies.

Place:

3.12 The next P of the marketing mix is Place or Distribution-reaching the offering to the consumer. Making the product accessible/available to the target customers at the time they want in quantities they want and offering other services are the main functions of distribution.

3.13 Companies have different distribution channels available to them based on customers, products and services required. Major distribution channel members used by different industries are:

- Warehouses or depots
- Distributors or stockists
- Dealers or retailers
- Franchisees etc.

As stated earlier, the primary functions of the distribution channel members are to make the product available to the customers as and when they want and render other after-sales services.

3.14 With increasing diversity of customers, products and geographic spread, companies need to have an efficient system to reach all its customers. In the process, they have to ensure total co-operation from channel members which itself will be a competitive advantage.

3.15 With recent advances in internet and other related technologies, on-line marketing is growing fast posing threat to organised and unorganised retail settings.

Promotion:

3.16 The final P - Promotion is as important as the other three Ps of the marketing mix though it is often misunderstood to be the only function of marketing. The primary purpose of promotion is to communicate about the company's offerings to consumers and get them interested in these.

3.17 Towards this end, companies use a mix of "pull" and "push" strategies - drawing the consumers to company's offerings on one hand and pushing them through channel members towards the consumers. It is a mix of advertising and other sales promotions measures.

3.18 Advertising plays a role in each stage of consumers' purchase process consisting of

- Awareness
- Interest
- Understanding
- Attitude
- Purchase and
- Repurchase

This is called the AIUAPR model of consumer purchase process.

3.19 The two dimensions of advertising are the message and the media – both depend on the product positioning strategy of the company. Usually, companies employ services of specialist advertising agencies in this regard. They will be advising the company on appropriate message and media decisions. The message could communicate functional and emotional benefits through an appropriate theme that appeals to target audience.

3.20 The primary media used are:

- TV
- Print which includes dailies, weekly and monthly magazines in English and vernacular languages
- Radio
- Outdoor media like hoardings, banners, posters at the point of sale etc.
- Again today, online and social media are extensively used in promoting brands.

3.21 There are several types of sales promotion which are normally oriented towards achieving short term objectives. These include

- Consumer offers
- Dealer offers and
- Sales force offers

3.22 Personal selling is a powerful sales promotional strategy and continues to be the backbone in selling and promotional efforts in many organisations. We say that everyone in the organisation including the CEO is a salesperson projecting the appropriate image of the company and its offerings to customers.

4.   Managing customer relations, managing brands and communication:

4.1   While the marketing mix framework is a comprehensive tool for developing marketing strategies, recent complexities pose great challenges to marketing to keep pace with change.

4.2   With explosive growth in technologies relating to information and communication, manufacturing etc., liberalisation and globalisation of national economies and constantly changing external environment, marketers are not able to predict and plan for the future with any great certainty as before. Environmental volatility, changing consumer perceptions and behaviour and international competition- all these call for new thinking, new insights and new strategies from marketers all the time. Unlike earlier stable times when customers were taken for granted, the challenge today is how to build and sustain competitive advantage.

4.3   In this constantly evolving competitive environment, the only way companies can hope to keep their customers happy and loyal is through building and maintaining long lasting relationships with customers. Maintaining and further strengthening relationships with the customers at personal level, at brand level and constantly maintaining two-way communication with them are the major tools available to companies to keep their customers with them and continue to grow in these turbulent times.

4.4   Thus, the major tools available to marketers to keep the customer engaged in today's dynamic marketing environment are:

• Customer Relationship Management (CRM) practices

• Strategic brand building and

• Integrated marketing communication systems.

Only companies that manage to build lasting relationships and trust with customers will be able to win in the long run. Each occasion when the customer comes in contact with the brand or company's offering is called the "moment of truth" and companies need to constantly create and reinforce the positive image of the company's brand on each occasion.

4.5   The current trend in marketing is to link "positioning" with "perception" by moving away from purely focusing on features and benefits to focus on enriching total "customer experiences". This is called "experiential marketing".

4.6   Further with explosive growth of Information and Communication Technologies (ICT), consumers and consumer (social) networks have become partners and co-creators of company's offerings.

5.   Developing competitive strategies:

5.1   Companies constantly evaluate their marketing strategies as reflected in their annual marketing plans which document company's plans for the coming year.

5.2   In this effort, companies need to revisit the following questions always and develop their dynamic market responses in terms of their strategy:

- Who are our customers and how do we serve them? - Customer orientation

- How do we define our markets? – Customer needs and wants

- Which market segments do we serve? – Segmentation, targeting and positioning (STP)

- What are our far and near environment considerations? – Environmental and competitor analysis

- What is our marketing mix? – 4 Ps framework

- What is the life cycle stage of our products? – New product development plans

- How do we add value to our customers? Company? – Customer value analysis and profitability analysis of our product portfolio.

- What do customers think of us? – Company and brand image, customer relations and communication

- What are our new marketing plans? – Profit, market share objectives and strategies

5.3 Product/Market development: We have seen that products follow a life cycle with introduction, growth, maturity and decline stages and profits from them also follow a similar pattern. In order to achieve our growth objectives in terms of profits, sales and market share, we need to decide where to put our promotional money and keep developing new products. There are generally four paths to achieve this:

- Greater market penetration – existing products, existing markets
- Product development – new products, existing markets
- Market development – existing products, new markets
- Diversification – new products, new markets

These are developed by a 2x2 matrix, called Ansoff matrix, named after Russian mathematician. However, defining what exactly you mean by products and markets is a challenging task and is subject to different interpretations. Also, this does not consider competitive scenario.

Hence, this decision is based largely on the overall corporate strategy of whether the corporation would pursue any/all of these approaches based on its analysis of general business as well as industry environment and its own resources and capabilities.

5.4 All we can say at this stage as a summary is that marketing is a cross-functional discipline and everyone in the organisation has a role to play in its efforts to offer customer satisfaction and delight so that they stay with the company and its offerings. This is the ultimate objective of marketing- creating and keeping a loyal customer.

Block 4: Human Resources Management

1. Understanding human behaviour:

1.1 As we have seen, management is essentially a social activity consisting of working with and through other people. Integrating and improving performance of other people is at the core of every manager's job. As such the first step to become a successful manger is to understand the behaviour of people working with you, motivating them for high performance, managing their performance and helping them develop themselves for moving on to positions of even greater responsibility. Thus, you evolve into a leader.

1.2 We need to understand human behaviour at individual, group and organisation levels for improving the performance of the organisation as a whole.

1.3 At the individual level, our behaviour depends on several factors as follows:

- Biographical characteristics like age, sex etc.
- Abilities
- Values
- Attitudes
- Personality type
- Learning style
- Emotions and
- Perceptions

1.4 Our personality type and learning style dictate how we communicate, relate to others, solve problems and learn. They are measured through personality and learning style inventories, ability tests etc.

1.5 To understand other people's behaviour, we need to appreciate their point of view. You also need to see how it is dictated by social pressures, conventions etc.

1.6 The rationalist view states that human behaviour depends on one's own mental models, values and goals.

1.7 Also there are social pressures which make us play our roles as per the rules of the game. We need to guard ourselves against being judgmental in understanding others' behaviour.

1.8 Interpersonal relationships take place in one-to-one relationships. Transactional Analysis (TA) framework developed by Dr Eric Berne, Canadian-born Psychiatrist states that we are a complex and shifting combination of three distinct sub-personalities -

- Parent
- Adult and
- Child

We take on these sub-personalities on different occasions. Thus, in a one-to-one relationship, the two parties involved, can take on different sub-personalities resulting in the following relationships:

- Adult to adult
- Parent to child
- Child to parent

- Child to child

An adult-to-adult relationship is generally healthy in work situations.

1.9 Moving on to group behaviour, we can say that people are inherently sociable and when they work together a social dynamic is created. This becomes more complex as more and more people get involved as in an organisational setting.

1.10 While the terms groups and teams are interchangeably used, teams are special groups. In teams,

- Each member has a specific role
- The members' work is interdependent and
- They work towards a common goal.

1.11 Factors external to the group that affect group effectiveness are:

- Size of the group
- Composition
- Task assigned
- Resources provided and
- Recognition awarded for the group's work

These are decided by outside people, generally by senior management.

1.12 The internal factors that affect group performance primarily depend on:

- The style of leadership provided
- Patterns of interactions among group members and

- Attention given by leadership to tasks, processes as well as to maintaining morale, commitment and cohesion of the group.

1.13 Some of the problems associated with group work are:

- Individual members pursuing their hidden agendas,
- Entire group getting unduly anxious over the task or
- All members beginning to think alike without bringing in their own valid perspectives thereby ignoring adverse signals

These lead to sub-optimal functioning and non-achievement of group's objectives.

1.14 For effective teamwork, there are certain team member roles to be played and an ideal team should have a mix of people with appropriate temperaments to play the different roles effectively. These roles include:

- Coordinator
- Plant
- Shaper
- Motivator
- Implementer
- Team worker
- Completer/finisher etc.

1.15 Teams go through turbulent stages of forming and norming (assigning tasks to individual members) before they start performing effectively.

1.16 While there are bound to be conflicts and disagreements in group work, establishing and clarifying individual goals and developing mutual trust will go a long way in resolving conflicts and enhancing group performance through achieving synergy.

1.17 Effective managers use their power, authority, and influence appropriately to influence positively members' performance and achieve desired results. Sources of power could be

- Position based
- Personality based or
- Expertise based

1.18 Based on our understanding of human behaviour, next step in managing people would be motivating them so that they get committed to their jobs and put in necessary efforts to achieve their job objectives and organisation's objectives. While there are several theories of motivation, in reality different combinations of them work in different situations. Performance of a person is directly related to his/her motivation apart from ability to do the job.

1.19 These models list out several motivational factors:

- Need hierarchy of human beings
- Hygiene and motivating factors
- Judgment of equity by the person
- Fulfillment of individual's expectations as the reward for job performance
- Participation in setting one's own goals
- individual's need for power, affiliation, achievement etc.

1.20 Individual job design based on a consideration of appropriate motivational factors will lead to high level of job performance.

1.21 Since human beings are essentially social animals, their social needs are to be fulfilled for achieving high performance levels apart from introduction of modern technological methods which reduce job strain and monotony considerably.

2. Leadership essentials:

2.1 The importance of leadership in running any organisation successfully cannot be overemphasised. Very often organisations succeed in their mission and continue to be successful largely due to the vision and direction provided by leadership. Similarly, most of corporate failures are largely due to failure of leadership.

2.2 Essentially leadership involves influencing others to follow a particular direction or goal.

2.3 Theories abound on leadership. These can be grouped in to:

•   Trait theories

•   Style theories and

•   Contingency theories

These attempt to list and explain characteristics of successful leaders. In practice, it is a mix of all the factors espoused by these theories that makes a great leader.

2.4 Trait theories list following traits among others, as those of successful leaders:

•   Intelligence

•   Dominance and self-confidence

- Interpersonal skills and

- An orientation towards achievement.

2.5 The managerial grid developed by Blake & Moulton, fits the various leadership styles in a two-by-two matrix along the two axes as follows:

- Concern for task and

- Concern for people

They are classified into impoverished management style (low concern for both task and people) to team management style (high concern for both task and people) as the preferred style. I have added one more dimension- Concern for processes as the third dimension. An ideal leadership should have high concern for tasks, people and processes in the three-dimensional model.

2.6 Another style theory by Tannenbaum and Schmidt plots various styles in a continuum from total use of authority by the leader at one end to total freedom to subordinates at the other end. In the former the leader/manager takes all decisions by him/her while in the latter, he/she gives total freedom to subordinates to function within limits dictated by the organisation in an objective manner. The various styles along the continuum can be termed as

- Tells

- Sells

- Tests

- Suggests

- Consults

- Joins and

- Delegates

2.7 Under contingency theory, the style of leadership is said to depend on the leader-member relations, task on hand and the position of power of the leader.

2.8 Broadly the leader's functions can be grouped into
- Strategic function
- Task function and
- Interpersonal function

2.9 Under his/her strategic role, leader sets the direction and leads the organisation in this direction.

2.10 He/she defines the tasks to be carried out in achieving company's vision and goals, finds necessary resources and ensures that the tasks are carried out effectively. This is the "means and ends" function.

2.11 Ensuring commitment of members to organisation's vision, maintaining the morale, cohesion and commitment are at the heart of leader's interpersonal role.

2.12 Following these, one can say that the major difference between a leader and a manger is that the former sets the direction, creates the goals to achieve this vision and gains the commitment of members to this shared vision and goals while the latter follows this direction, organises and co-ordinates people and resources to achieve the given goals. Thus, a leader is an innovator and developer with a bias towards action while a manager is an administrator and a maintenance person.

2.13 However to be successful, a manager should evolve into a leader by developing holistic and creative thinking skills, motivating skills and long-term thinking skills. They have to become great communicators, act as role models and develop action orientation.

2.14 This leads to the communication skills necessary to become a successful leader/manager since it is only through communication that one can solicit and elicit necessary enthusiasm and commitment to clearly articulated goals and vision. They have to develop their oral, written as well as non-verbal communication skills. While threshold level communication skills are necessary for all jobs, leaders need to become great communicators. Of course, the other half of communicating effectively is listening well. This requires the leader to listen attentively to what the other person says and understands his/her message fully.

3. Managing performance and development:

3.1 Human Resources Management (HRM) processes consist of managing entry, performance and development through well-established systems and practices.

3.2 The various steps involved in managing entry consists of: analysing manpower requirements, recruitment, selection, induction and socialisation.

3.3 We need to develop job descriptions for individual jobs considering short-term and long-term requirements, organisational environment and need for any change in the current job profile.

3.4 We then look around for a suitable candidate based on his/her fit for both the job and organisation through the recruitment process consisting of calling for applications through various sources.

3.5   The next step of selection is normally done through a series of processes consisting of checking the applicant's background in terms of qualifications and experience relevant to the job as given in his/her application, personal interviews etc. to assess the candidate's suitability. One needs to take care to verify information provided as well as overcome personal biases/prejudices during the interview/ selection process.

3.6   Finally, the new recruit is inducted into the organisation and new role through effective formal induction and socialisation processes.

3.7   As an ongoing activity, providing effective supervision is a major process in HRM. Very often the immediate supervisor is the first point of formal contact with the organisation and his/her behaviour is the major cause for an employee's performance as well as satisfaction or dissatisfaction with the job and organisation.

3.8   As his/her primary responsibility, the supervisor performs task and maintenance functions. Task related activities are towards ensuring that targets set are understood and achieved while the supervisor maintains the morale, cohesion and commitment of his group through people related activities.

3.9   In managing individual's performance, as we have seen earlier the manager has to set SMART (simple, measurable, agreed, realistic and timed) objectives and also standards of performance and measures should be set and explained.

3.9   Performance should be periodically assessed objectively, and corrective actions taken in terms of counseling and formal appraisal sessions.

3.10 In the case of under-performing employees, following steps need to be taken:

- Identify and agree on the problem
- Establish reasons for under performance-lack of support, skills, ability, attitude etc.
- Decide on required action and resource the action like coaching, training etc.
- Monitor and provide feedback on an agreed periodic basis

3.11 An important aspect of performance management is pay and reward systems. Ranking of jobs to fix salary levels and monitoring market continuously to know industry and competitor salary structure are some of the essential steps in updating company's pay and reward system.

3.12 People look for equity in their pay structure in terms of fairness of rewards in relation to their input efforts compared to that of others. Hence any pay and reward system should be based on this consideration. Often, non-monetary rewards play an important role in providing that extra motivation.

3.13 As a manager, you have an important role to play in the development of your subordinates. Apart from being a role model, you will be in a position to coach them as well as providing opportunities for other learning avenues.

3.14 Normally, management training and development programs aim to develop certain skills and competencies in selected individuals to enable them to perform better in their current assignments as well as preparing them for positions of greater responsibilities in future.

3.15 Training programs aim to develop certain specific skills while development programs aim to develop a wider thinking horizon preparing the participant to think beyond current position and develop new competencies for superior job performance today and in future.

3.16 Some of the options used in training and development are:

- Coaching
- Mentoring
- Job rotations
- Special assignments
- Sponsorship to special internal and external programs

3.17 Developing your own self is primarily your responsibility and you need to keep expanding your skills and knowledge base to move up further in your career. You need to become a reflective practitioner and lifelong learner. You also have to learn to handle stress and achieve right degree of work-life balance for a happy living.

3.18 While good "IQ" and technical skills are threshold capabilities to perform well in a managerial job, you need to develop a high degree of "Emotional intelligence – EQ" to become an effective leader.

3.19 The components of emotional intelligence are: self-awareness and self-regulation (managing self), motivation (a strong will to achieve), empathy and social skills (capacity to manage relationships).

3.20 You also need to find out your niche strength which can become your career anchor. It could be technical competence, service/dedication, entrepreneurial spirit, love for pure challenge etc.

3.21 Organisations need to create conditions conducive to lifelong learning for all its members. It then becomes a learning organisation where failures are tolerated, lessons are learnt from these failures and new innovative thinking is encouraged and rewarded.

4. Managing change:

4.1 Since external environment is dynamic and keeps changing, individuals and organisations need to be sensitive to these changes and be ready to adapt to emerging opportunities and threats.

4.2 When an organisation faces the challenge of change, one has to look at

- People
- Structure
- Systems and
- Tasks involved

All these are interconnected and change in any one of these impacts all the other factors. Hence the extent of change has to be planned considering its impact on all factors.

4.3 The change process consists of three stages as follows:

- Unfreezing where existing practices are discarded,
- Changing when required changes are implemented and
- Refreezing where the changed practices become the way of doing things.

4.4 Major change strategies include:

- Directive strategies
- Educative strategies and
- Participative strategies

The appropriate strategy is chosen considering the urgency of the situation and the nature of tasks, people, structure and systems as seen above. Companies need to create the right kind of climate for change for any lasting impact.

4.5   Several steps are to be taken at each stage of the change process- preparing for change, implementing change and consolidating change.

Block 5: Financial Management

Importance of Finance: In running an organisation all resources, investments, incomes, expenses etc. are measured in financial terms. The basic purpose of any organisation is to make profits and add on to the wealth of promoters which are again measured in money terms. Thus, finance is the common yardstick for evaluating performance and as such, managers need to understand basics of finance to perform effectively.

1. Understanding financial statements:

1.1 The two fundamental financial statements are the Balance Sheet and the Profit and Loss (PL) or Income Statement. While the former gives the financial position of the organisation as on a given time, the latter indicates the financial performance over a period of time, normally one year. These are based on certain generally accepted accounting concepts, norms, conventions, policies and judgments.

1.2 Some of the major accounting concepts and conventions are:

- Firm as a separate entity - It is separate from the owners

- Money as common measurement - Everything gets measured in monetary value

- Firm as going concern - The firm is assumed to be in business and is expected to continue in business as a running organisation

- Dual aspect - Every transaction will affect two sides- credit and debit

- Matching sources and uses - These should balance out
- Accounting on accrual basis - All incomes, expenses etc. are recorded as when they are incurred

1.3 Balance sheet is based on the dual aspect of the firm. It represents resources owned by the firm (assets) as equal to claims of parties on the assets of the firm (liabilities).

1.4 Assets consist of long-term fixed assets and short-term current assets.

1.5 Liabilities to shareholders consist of equity and retained earnings while debt represents what is owed to outsiders. Together, they make up the total liabilities of the firm.

1.6 Income statement presents the incomes for a given period (usually one year) in terms of sales revenue and other income. On the expenses side, we include raw material costs, wages, overhead expenses, interest, depreciation etc.

1.7 If total income for a given period exceeds total expenditure, the firm makes a profit for that accounting period. If reverse is the case, the firm makes a loss.

2. Financial ratio analysis:

2.1 Mere absolute numbers of profits, income, expenditure etc. by themselves may not reveal how effectively and efficiently the firm makes use of its resources. Hence, we use financial ratios to measure performance.

2.2 Major financial measures used in performance analysis are: capital structure, assets deployment, liquidity, utilisation, expenses, profitability etc.

2.3 Financial ratios used for these performance measures are:

- Capital structure: Debt / equity ratio
- Assets deployment: Fixed assets / long term funds
    Current assets / total assets
    Inventory / current assets
    Receivables / current assets
    Cash / current assets
- Liquidity: Current assets / current liabilities
- Utilisation: Sales / total assets
    Sales / fixed assets
    Sales / current assets
    Sales / inventories
    Sales / receivables

2.4 Operating cycle is an important measure of utilisation. It measures how long it takes for the firm to turn around or receive the cash invested in raw materials etc. back as cash. Each item of expenditure is expressed as a percentage of sales to analyse and control performance in that area.

2.5 There are several measures to analyse profitability in terms of return on sales, return on equity, return on investment etc.

2.6 A major framework for analysing financial performance is the Du Pont control chart which measures profitability from shareholders' point of view which is Profit after tax (PAT) / equity. It helps in analysing the three critical areas of performance drivers which are:

- Cost management measured by Profit after tax (PAT) / Sales. How well you are managing your costs
- Asset management measured by Sales / Total assets. How well you are managing your assets
- Leverage management measured by Total assets / Equity. How well you are leveraging your equity

The equation representing these measurements is as follows:

Profit after tax (PAT) / Equity = PAT / Sales x Sales / Total assets x Total assets / Equity

Return on shareholder equity is driven by cost management, assets management and leverage management.

2.7   Other measures used to analyse firm's performance from shareholder's point of view are:

Earnings per share (EPS) = Net earnings of the company for each share.

Price earnings ratio (PE ratio) = Market price of share / Net earnings per share and

Dividend yield = Dividend declared per share / Current share price.

These measures are used since shareholders look for both short term dividend payouts as well as long term appreciation of their share value in the stock market.

2.8   Other tools used for financial control are funds flow and cash flow statements which analyse sources and uses of funds.

Taken together, these measures indicate the financial status of the company.

3. Understanding costs and budgets:

3.1 Cost accounting plays an important role in financial control of the firm and helps in making following major decisions:

- Determining and controlling costs and finalising prices
- Determining cost, price, and volume relationship through sensitivity analysis
- Make or buy decisions
- Preventing fraud

3.2 In the classic cost centre approach, costs for each cost centre are worked out and costs are apportioned to various products based on utilisation of these cost centre activities by each product. The total cost for the product will include

- Primary costs consisting of direct material cost and direct wages
- Manufacturing overheads based on above allocation
- Selling and distribution overheads

3.3 To arrive at break-even point (the point at which no profits or no losses are made) and have a flexible marginal approach to costing and pricing, we use the concept of fixed costs, variable costs and break-even analysis. Contribution is defined as selling price – variable costs, which goes towards meeting the fixed costs of the company. The break-even volume or value of sales is the point at which all costs, fixed and variable, are fully met and there is no loss or profit. Beyond this, each unit sold gives contribution which becomes profit. This enables companies to take flexible decisions on pricing beyond break-even volumes when they have adequate capacity to meet additional demand.

3.4 In order to control costs and ensure that financial objectives are achieved, firms have strong budgeting control systems and review processes to take necessary corrective measures.

3.5 These basically study the variances between budgets and actuals and analyse the causes for these variances to take corrective measures.

3.6 Budgets also indicate the financial resources required and allocation of these resources for achievement of company's financial and other objectives for the future.

4. Understanding shareholder value:

4.1 The primary objective of any firm is to create shareholder value.

4.2 This value could be realized either by dividends or appreciation of value of capital (share price).

4.3 Firms strive to control following value drivers to realize their objectives:

On the revenue side: customer mix, product mix, productivity, quality etc.

On the cost side: fixed costs, variable costs, overhead costs etc.

4.4 A major concept used in understanding value creation is time value of money. It states that while investing in projects, earlier the cash inflows are realized, higher is the present value of the project. All projected future cash flows are discounted to present value by using a discount rate which is the cost of capital of the firm, which is the weighted cost of equity and debt.

4.5 Based on this concept, following measures are used in evaluating value performance of the firm and future projects:

- Net present value (NPV)
- Internal rate of return (IRR)
- Economic value added (EVA)

4.6 In order to direct the efforts of the organisation towards fulfillment of expectations of all stakeholders, a comprehensive performance measuring concept called Balanced Scorecard is used. Under this, firms establish objectives, measures, targets and initiatives to fulfill firms' vision under four perspectives:

- Financial perspective
- Customer perspective
- Internal business processes perspective
- Learning and growth perspective

4.7 With increasing awareness among general and investing public, companies are resorting to newer measures to present their performance reports. Some of the major frameworks incorporating these measures are:

- ESG: Environmental, Social and Governance metrics for measuring a company's ability to create long term value for investors
- TPL: Triple Bottom Line accounting framework for measuring social, environmental and financial performance

Block 6: Managing Operations and the Supply Chain

1. Managing the steady state in Operations and support functions:

1.1   Manufacturing as a function has come a long way from being one with narrow focus looking at only producing or manufacturing to encompassing all operations that take place inside the company. It has now further extended to entire supply chain starting from raw material vendors to reaching the customers and trade channels. Truly, operations function is the backbone of any organisation.

1.2   With increased global access to customers and suppliers while facing global competition, companies need to improve their manufacturing performance on a continuous basis to remain relevant and maintain their competitive advantage.

1.3   Operations function takes care of the following flows and systems in the organisation:

- Physical transformation system converting inputs to desired outputs through a transformation process
- The information processing system translating and executing customer orders to their fulfillment and
- Accounting/costing inputs for managing revenues and costs.

Like all management functions, it is also an integrative one.

1.4   Managing performance in operations involves maintaining steady state and conformance with respect to following:

- Product specifications
- Quality
- Quantity
- Cost
- Timely supplies etc. as desired by customers

1.5   This calls for corrective actions within the existing system to meet the performance changes required by changes in external environment or internal systems.

1.6   Output objectives change due to changes in market conditions reflected in customer demand. Often there is a conflict between output objectives and resource utilisation objectives. Further, maintenance and renewal of resources also interrupt steady state and pose challenges to steady state conformance.

1.7   Production systems in an organisation depend on the following:
- Nature of demand for its products
- Technology used in terms of manufacturing and information
- Production control systems and
- Type of organisation

1.8   Depending on above factors, production system could be
- Jobbing
- Batch production
- Mass production
- Continuous flow
- Combination of the above

1.9 With explosion in information technology, production control systems are becoming more and more sophisticated based on integrating information from customer order through the supply chain until orders are fulfilled. Some of the modern sophisticated production control systems are:

- Material Resource Planning (MRP)
- Just in Time (JIT) manufacturing
- Optimised production Technology (OPT)

1.10 With the emergence of marketing concept, the driving force behind operations systems is meeting the needs of the customers competitively in terms of quality, quantity, time (timely deliveries) and cost. Earlier the primary focus was on maximising production output for achieving the most efficient use of resources. This calls for shifting the management style from "control" to "commitment".

1.11 Companies need to have robust control systems for other functions supporting production/manufacturing. These include

- Purchase and inventory control
- Quality control
- Manpower control
- Maintenance control
- Cost control etc.

2. Continuous performance improvement:

2.1 Through constant incremental and disruptive innovation companies keep improving their performance to maintain their competitive advantage.

2.2 The concept of continuous performance improvement became popular largely due to emergence of Japanese way of management in general, and manufacturing management in particular, which helped Japanese automobile industry overtake the established American auto industry.

2.3 Japanese call it "Kaizen" which means gradual, unending improvement, doing little things better, setting and achieving even higher standards.

2.4 Several areas come under the kaizen umbrella:
   • Customer focus
   • Quality control
   • Small group activities
   • Productivity improvements etc.

2.5 JIT (Just in Time) is the process adopted by Japanese companies to bring in continuous productivity improvements. These are aimed at improving production and productivity continuously to move towards eliminating inventories, rejects etc. to ensure minimal lead time between receipt of customer orders and execution.

2.6 OPT (Optimised Production technology) is another productivity improvement system which relates profits to increasing throughput while reducing inventories and operational expenses through synchronised production.

2.7 Quality improvement systems are based on the philosophy that quality means conformance to customer requirements and is the responsibility of everyone in the organisation. Six Sigma is a process which aims to minimise and eliminate errors and deviations completely in various processes and systems.

2.8 Japanese ways of technical improvement include improving individual operations, improving factory layout and through housekeeping programs.

2.9 Improvements in human resource performance are brought about by job enlargement (increasing breadth of jobs to include more responsibilities), job enrichment (increasing depth of jobs to make them more responsible and meaningful) etc. to provide greater motivation.

2.10 Flexibility in operations is another key factor to bring in continuous improvement. This calls for creation of slack resources to meet unexpected surges in demand, creation of tasks that are self-contained, maintenance of healthy labour relations and robust information systems.

2.11 Cellular Manufacturing concept is widely used in modern manufacturing organisations where tasks are allotted to small groups or cells so that they will have autonomy and better control on their own activities.

2.12 With increasing awareness and concern over environmental degradation, yet another emerging concept is Circular Manufacturing. Here the efforts are to maximise recirculation of all waste and leftovers back into the manufacturing system under a regenerative model to minimize wastage.

3. Managing the supply chain:

3.1 In the last two decades, Supply Chain Management has become a key area to gain competitive advantage especially for global companies. Focus of operations management has shifted from quality management to manufacturing efficiency improvement to supply chain management.

3.2 A supply chain consists of all parties involved directly or indirectly in fulfilling a customer order. Several parties known as supply chain members from raw material manufacturers to final retail dealers play an important part in meeting the customer demand for on time supplies at minimum costs. Managing the relationships between all these members is the primary responsibility of the supply chain manager.

3.3 Materials, information, finance- all flow along the supply chain. The objective of every supply chain is to minimize costs along the chain and at the same time ensure timely deliveries to offer better value to customers than competition.

3.4 Depending on the nature of the product, a suitable supply chain is designed and monitored. For products which are innovative, have a short life cycle and demand is uncertain, supply chain will have to be designed based on providing quick response time to customer needs.

3.5 For functional products with stable demand but uncertain supply conditions, supply chain is designed to minimize risks of disruption in supplies.

3.6 For stable demand and supply situations, efficiency becomes the primary focus to minimize costs. This is achieved by eliminating non-value adding activities and better co-ordination among members.

3.7 Thus, managing the supply chain is a cross functional activity and calls for coordination among all functions.

4. Key emerging technologies:

4.1 Several emerging technologies are fundamentally changing the way people live, work and play, giving new experience to consumers and making living easier and more enjoyable. The rate of growth of these technologies seems unprecedented. New developments are taking place at a breakneck speed and organisations and managers are barely able to keep up with the latest developments which are truly disruptive.

4.2 With very high computing power and access to large data bases, machines are fast learning to outperform human beings in many spheres and are becoming more and more "intelligent". Some of the key emerging technologies arising out of this are listed below:

- Artificial Intelligence (AI)
- Internet Of Things (IOT)
- 3D Printing
- Robotics and Robotic Process Automation (RPA)
- Blockchain
- Augmented and Virtual Reality (AR and VR)

In major developed economies, these technologies are already causing major disruptions in many industries and the race is on between companies to acquire, develop and apply these to their day-to-day operations to stay ahead of competition.

Primary reference books

1.   Study Materials for B-800: Foundations of Senior Management by the Open University Business School, UK

2.   Marketing 3.0: From Products to Customers to the Human Spirit (2010) by Philip Kotler, Hermawan and Iwan Setiawan

3.   Marketing Management: A South Asian Perspective (13th Edition - 2009) by Philip Kotler, Kevin Lane Keller, Abraham Koshy and Mithileshwar Jha

4.   Strategic Brand Management: Building, Measuring and Managing Brand Equity (2nd Edition - 2007) by Kevin Lane Keller

5.   Mastering Management 2.0: Your Single-Source Guide to Becoming a Master of Management by Financial Times: Edited by James Pickford (2004)

6.   Organisational behaviour (11th Edition - 2006) by Stephen P. Robbins and Seema Sanghi

7.   Key management ratios: The 100+ ratios every manager needs to know (Fourth edition - 2008) by Ciaran Walsh

8.   Contemporary Strategy Analysis (Third Edition-1998) by Robert M. Grant

Afterword

I started writing the booklet on Basics of Business Management and subsequent booklets covering each block by end of 2019. So far, I have completed four booklets and two more remain. The Covid 19 pandemic hit the world right through this period of end 2019, whole of 2020, 2021 and third and fourth waves are on us right now since January 2022. It has shaken the very basics of our lives to a great extent. As a consequence, whatever is written here has to be seen in this changed context. While all the basic and classic ideas presented here are equally applicable in the present circumstances, we need to modify the ways in which we apply them in the present context.

For example, work from home and online meetings have become the new norms in inter and intra office meetings involving white collar jobs. However, one can see a yearning as well as reluctance to get back to normalcy as soon as possible with abatement of the pandemic. Similarly, the phenomenal growth of online shopping has changed the ways in which products are promoted, stored, bought and delivered. These have given way to new business opportunities and have also led to the demise of many established ones. Integrated global supply chains are fraying at their ends to meet the supplies and demands from various parts of the world.

Driving all these is the relentless growth of the digital technologies. While this has brought in several advantages, it has also created many challenges. Navigating business in the digital world is the basic challenge faced by all companies and their managers.

With greater penetration of social media, people in all countries have become more aware of developments all over the world. As seen earlier, this has revolutionised the way people see and buy products and services. Brand loyalty based purely on premium image by multinational corporations (MNCs) is taking a beating with the emergence of "value for money" shift in consumer's minds. While more avenues for finance are available, pressures to control costs and offer robust profits to shareholders are proving to be great challenges in managing the finances of organisations.

Further, this has also brought in greater awareness among people on growing inequalities. It is an established fact that the rich, especially the very rich, have grown disproportionately rich and the poor, the bottom of the pyramid, have become poorer. Women empowerment as well as emerging groups like LGBT (lesbian, gay, bisexual and transgender) all need recognition and expect acceptance and opportunities available to others. Organisations cannot just stop at paying lip service to the concept of 'equal opportunity employer' but need to implement the same in letter and spirit.

In the current global political scenario, the so-called "superpowers" are flexing their muscles and are becoming more and more protective of their industries and territories. Emerging nations, having suffered suppression by them are also jostling for niche space more vigorously. A unipolar world that existed with the demise of Soviet Union is once again witnessing great rivalries between the two economic superpowers of USA and China. Both of them and Russia are vying to be the leader in the global context with financial, trade and military might and unbridled ambition for expanding their territories and spheres of influence. These conflicts have created great tension and flareup among them and other nations which have aligned with them all over the world. At the same time, threat of nuclear warfare by any indiscriminate ruler in any one of these countries hangs heavily in the air and the United Nations has been reduced to a mute spectator. These have led to authoritarian leaders in many countries and democratic values and freedom of thought and expression have been curtailed.

How true this has played out is being seen by the unexpected invasion of Ukraine by Russia, started in February 2022. This war has been dragging on till today causing much human misery and disturbing the whole world with prospects of massive hunger caused by sudden breakdown of supply chains. The comity of nations is getting fractured, and the threat of nuclear warfare appears real. As far as business and management fields are concerned, companies have gone back to drawing boards to rewrite their supply chain configurations even as they have just started implementing new supply chain strategies as a fallout of Covid 19. Once again, inequalities are rising and while new millionaires are springing up fast, millions of people are staring at abject poverty.

With the devastating blow delivered by Covid 19, governments have once again become the major economic engines in most of these nations. Giant technological corporations that dominate the digital world are fighting fiercely to protect their turfs as well as make inroads into others' domains. In the process, they are dictating the ways we, the people, live since our modern lives depend on them. Governments are finding it more and more difficult to rein them in due to their financial and market powers.

Most of the world is facing the reality of environmental degradation and the growing green movement to protect the globe for the present and future generations is gathering force.

All these have naturally affected all organisations' priorities, objectives, strategies etc.

Summing up, we can say that "business as usual" or old ways of doing things will not work anymore. New, innovative ways need to be found to meet these challenges constantly in this ever-changing scenario. However, I would like to emphasise that these basic, classic concepts and ideas still hold good, and we need to modify the ways we practise them. The basic purpose of these booklets is to expose the readers to all these classic concepts that have stood the test of time in a simple and concise manner so that they can start thinking and working out how to put them in practice in the current context.

A.S. Srinivasan   **October, 2022**

A.S. Srinivasan

A.S. Srinivasan holds a bachelor's degree in Mechanical Engineering (from the University of Madras), a Post Graduate Diploma in Plastics Engineering (D.I.I.T. from the Indian Institute of Technology, Bombay) and a Master's degree in Business Management (M.B.M. from the Asian Institute of Management, Manila, Philippines). He has participated in the Global Program for Management Development of the University of Michigan Business School.

Srinivasan has over 25 years of experience in industry and 15 years of experience in academics and consulting. His industry experience is primarily in the areas of Marketing and General Management in companies like TI Cycles, Aurofood, Pierce Leslie and Cutfast.

His last assignment was with Chennai Business School, a start up business school in Chennai, for over two years. As the first Dean of the school, he developed and implemented the curriculum for the post graduate program in management for the first batch. Prior to that, he was working with Institute for Financial Management and Research (IFMR), Chennai, for 8 years looking after the partnership with the Open University Business School (OUBS), UK in offering their Executive MBA in India. Apart from handling courses in the PGDM program of IFMR, he was actively involved in offering Management Development Programs (MDPs) to corporates and in consultancy assignments.

His current interests are in the areas of Management, Business, Economics etc. where he would like to keep himself updated with recent developments. He has taken to publishing blogs on these subjects for private circulation.

A.S. Srinivasan
A1/3/4, "Srinivas", Third Main Road,
Besant Nagar, Chennai 600 090
Mobile: 91 98414 01721
Email: sansrini@gmail.com

Printed in Great Britain
by Amazon

42530020R00036